P9-DGJ-820

RYE FREE READING ROOM

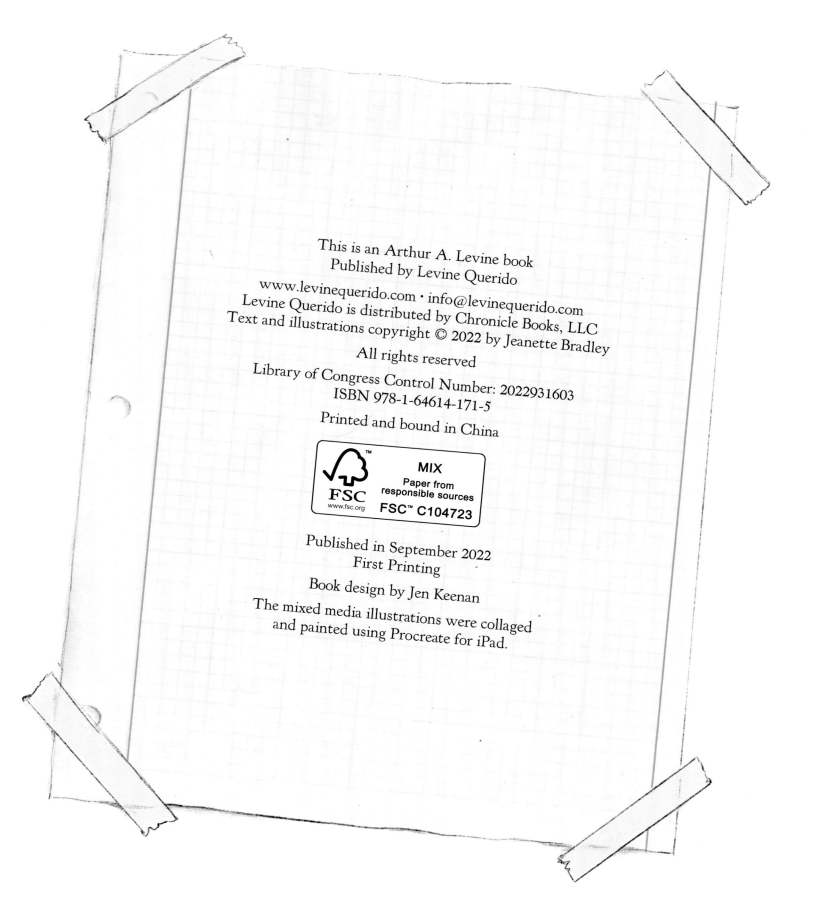

This is an Arthur A. Levine book
Published by Levine Querido

www.levinequerido.com · info@levinequerido.com
Levine Querido is distributed by Chronicle Books, LLC

Text and illustrations copyright © 2022 by Jeanette Bradley

All rights reserved

Library of Congress Control Number: 2022931603
ISBN 978-1-64614-171-5

Printed and bound in China

FSC
www.fsc.org

MIX
Paper from
responsible sources
FSC™ C104723

Published in September 2022
First Printing

Book design by Jen Keenan

The mixed media illustrations were collaged
and painted using Procreate for iPad.

Jeanette Bradley

LQ

LEVINE QUERIDO

Montclair | Amsterdam | Hoboken

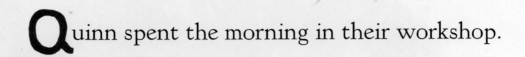

Quinn spent the morning in their workshop.

Finally, they made something that worked.
Something great, in fact.

Something Great could **tick-tock.**

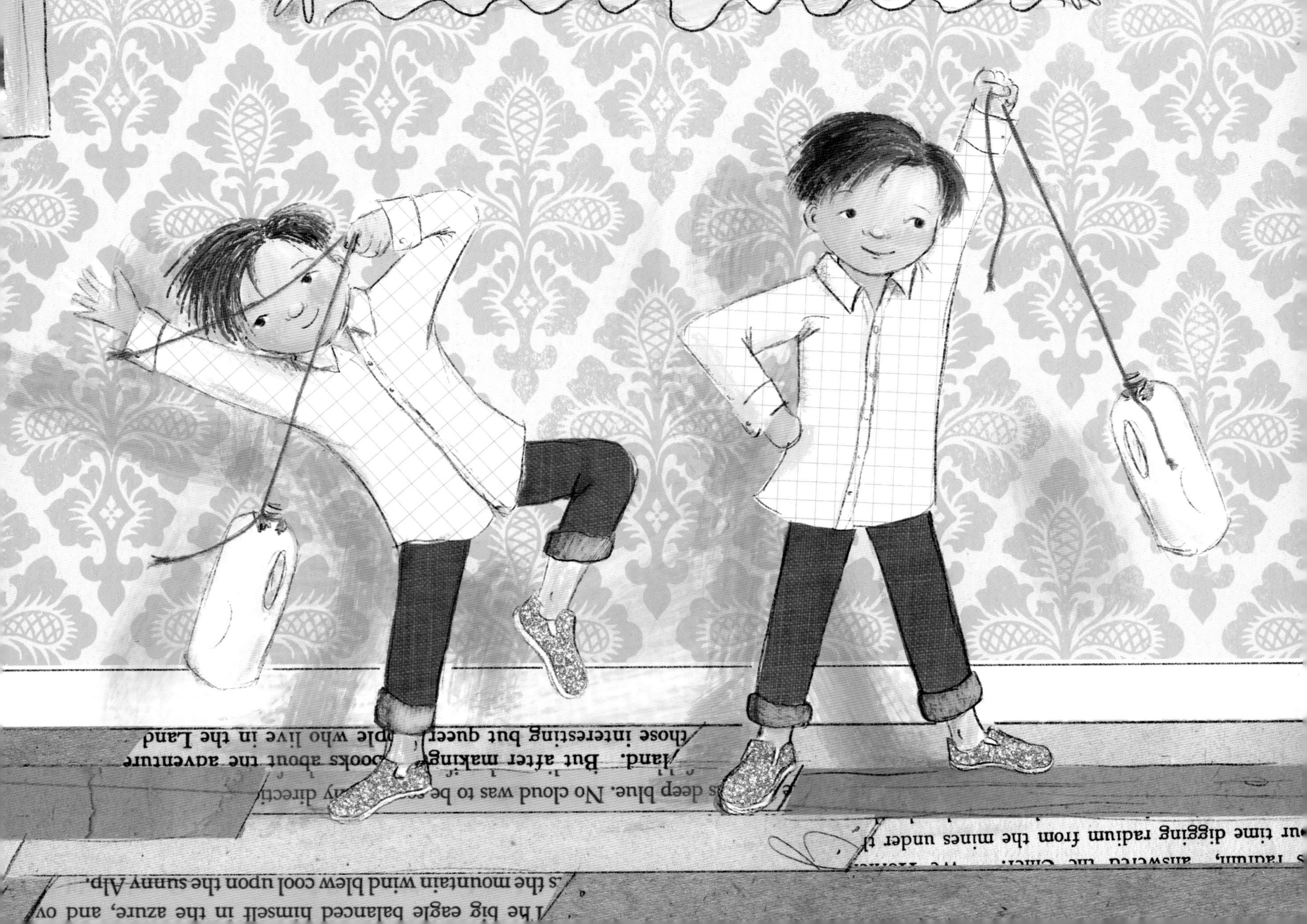

It could orbit around,

and around,

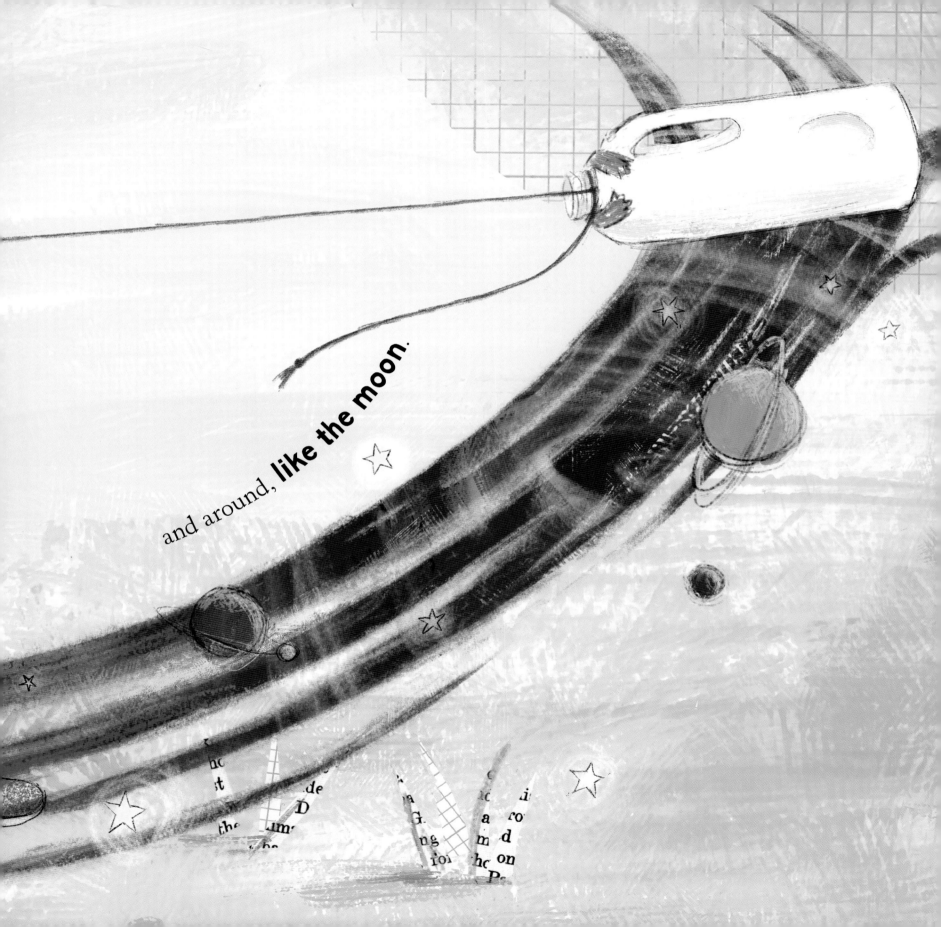

and around, **like the moon.**

Surprisingly, it could **sing**!

Quinn showed it to their big sister.

"What's that supposed to be?
Have you been playing in the recycling again?"

They showed it to their mother.

"That's wonderful honey, what's it supposed to be?"

Isis was only interested in the string.

Quinn flopped onto the grass. No one understood.
Something Great wasn't recycling!
And it wasn't supposed to be anything.
It was just . . .

. . . itself.

Something Great!

Quinn noticed that the sun made Something Great

glow with all the colors of the rainbow.

Quinn dropped in a stick.

Now Something Great had
shadow pictures inside.

It hung straight and
heavy in Quinn's hand.
As straight as . . .

"Hi," said a voice from above.

"What's that?"

"Um. Nothing.
Just something I made," said Quinn.

"Can I try?" asked the new kid. "All my stuff is in boxes."

"No, it cannot be Sir Lance... the king... sleeve emb...dere... treets; but if you entered one of... him to come to tak...ld find it bare and... When at last the tournamen... th... that the strange knight who... the with pearls had won the priz...

Something Great could **tick-tock** even better from up in the tree.
"This thing is the best!"

Quinn pulled down on the string.
Something Great went up.

When Quinn let go,
it came back down.

It could be an **elevator**!

Something Great could be so many great things: A **beat keeper**.

A **bug catcher**.

Or a **stick lifter**.

It might even be . . .

a friend

finder!